IFEO   geria.

After c   ndon,

she   don

Her first   r *Keeps* as

"like step   sunshine".

It was chosen by   n books of 1993,

and   994.

It was   g *Story*,

C   rs,

Or   and

My Grandf   rican Village.

D1390450

To the children of Senegal and Nigeria, for reminding me of my own childhood games

First published in Great Britain in 1999 by
Frances Lincoln Limited, 4 Torriano Mews
Torriano Avenue, London NW5 2RZ

First paperback edition 2000

British Library Cataloguing in Publication Data
available on request

ISBN hardback 0-7112-1279-1
ISBN paperback 0-7112-1471-9

Set in Angie

Printed in Hong Kong

9 8 7 6 5 4 3 2 1

Ebele's Favourite

A Book of African Games

IFEOMA ONYEFULU

FRANCES LINCOLN

AUTHOR'S NOTE

As a child growing up in Africa, playing was the most important part of my life. I loved inventing my own games using hibiscus leaves, and sometimes I cooked meals with pieces of paper, just like Ebele in this book. I enjoyed playing traditional games with my brothers, sister and friends, too. My own favourite games were Okoso and Oga.

I have grown up believing that children need to play. Some of the skills they will use later on in life are learnt by interacting with one another - following the rules, waiting their turn, and not cheating. The excitement of getting together, of encouraging the younger ones to join in, seems to me to be worth much more than winning.

Songs are essential to some of the games. You'll find translations at the back of the book. The words that go with Ryembalay are in the Wolof language of Senegal. The other songs are in Igbo, my own language.

My name is Ebele and I live
in Nigeria. I love playing games.
Sometimes I play from morning
till night, without even stopping
for a drink of water. I make meals
from pieces of paper, and eat
them sitting on the paper chair
I've made. They taste even better
than Mama's cooking!

But usually I play with my
friends. Our favourite place is the
ama – a big space in the middle of
our village where children can play
safely. Grown-ups use it, too, for
special meetings and festivals.

HOW TO PLAY

RYEMBALAY

(Round and round the garden like a teddy-bear) For this game you need 2 players. To win, you must try to tickle your friend to bits! Player 1 sings the song, then "walks" her fingers along the other player's arm, ending with a tickle. Then Player 2 takes her turn.

Last week, while I was busy playing, a letter arrived from Ngony, my Senegalese cousin. Ngony is coming to stay, and she wants to know my favourite game. "It will be fun to play our own special games," she writes.

Ngony's favourite game is *Ryembalay*. It's a tickling game. She likes to sing the Ryembalay Song:

Boula sa yaye mayé ...
Boula sa baye mayé ...
Boula sa mame mayé ...
Tanque ba gui – tanque ba gui
Fi la ko ame.

Ngony loves to tickle her friends to make them laugh. No wonder they call her "Laughter"!

Ngony has sent me photographs of herself, her brother Musa and a friend, in Dakar. Here they are playing Ryembalay, with Musa looking on.

I must decide quickly what is my favourite game. Ngony is coming in two weeks' time!

I like *Itu Okwe*, which is a throwing game – but I can't choose it because it is one of my brother Ugo's special games. Ugo is older than me, and he plays Itu Okwe for hours with his friends. In fact, they call him "the Longest Arms", because he plays it better than anyone else.

There's another game I really like. It's called *Okereke Okereke,* (Passing the Sticks). While we are playing it, we sing:

> *Okereke okereke dun dun du ya ya*
> *Okerafor okerafor dun dun du ya ya*
> *Kwena oganaga*

The trouble is, my brother Amaechi passes the sticks faster than anyone else – as fast as the snake Papa chased out of the house recently. So I suppose it's really Amaechi's special game, not mine.

HOW TO PLAY **OKEREKE OKEREKE** *(Passing the sticks)*

For this game, you need at least 8 players in a circle and a big handful of sticks. Everyone sings and passes the sticks one by one along the ground to the next person, getting faster and faster. If a player doesn't keep up with everyone else, he is out of the game. The last person left is the winner.

Perhaps I could choose *Okoso*, a spinning game – but not while Chima, my younger brother, is around! Chima is king of Okoso. The way he spins the top until it turns upside down, is pure magic! That's why his friends call him "the Whirlwind", after the wind that blows here on hot afternoons.

HOW TO PLAY **OKOSO** *(A spinning game)*
For this game you need at least 2 players and an old-fashioned spinning top. To win, you have to keep the top spinning longer than anyone else.

I certainly won't choose *Ncho*, a counting game, as my favourite, because Chima's best friend Okey plays it so well. No one has ever beaten him. Okey always thinks one step ahead. He knows when to stop to pick up his opponent's seeds and when to carry on to win lots more.

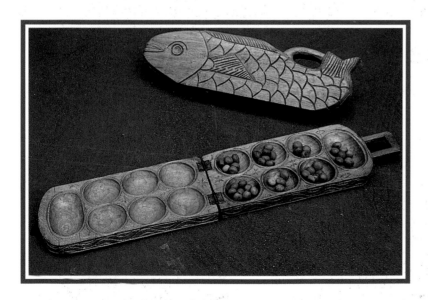

HOW TO PLAY

NCHO

For this game you need 2 players and a Ncho set. Put 4 seeds in each hollow. Each player chooses one row of 6 hollows to be his side. The hollows at each end are for storing seeds, not for playing.

Player 1 scoops up the seeds from any hollow on his side and moves around the board, dropping a seed in each hollow until he runs out. Then he scoops up the seeds where he has landed and goes on until he runs out again. When he lands on Player 2's side, he can either continue to move around the board, or he can take out the seeds and store them. If he decides to store them, it is then Player 2's turn. Player 2 plays in the same way, but moves the opposite way around the board. The winner is the person who collects most seeds.

I won't choose *Okwe*, (Knucklebones), either. It's Chi-Chi's favourite game. Chi-Chi is my best friend, and she plays Okwe much better than I do. In fact, she's the local champion, and she always scoops up more pebbles than anyone else. We call her *"Agu Nkwo"*, (a bird of prey), because she has sharp eyes and moves fast.

HOW TO PLAY

OKWE *(Knucklebones or Jacks)*

For this game you need at least 2 players and some pebbles or palm kernels. Player 1 throws a pebble into the air and has to pick up one or more pebbles before catching the first one. She stores the pebbles she catches and plays again. When she lets a pebble drop, she loses her turn. The person collecting most pebbles wins.

It's a pity I can't choose *Kpu kpun kpu ogene* (Crawling through the Passage). It's my friend Ify's special game. If I choose it, maybe she won't want me to be her partner next time we play it. While we're playing, we sing:

Kpu kpun kpu ogene
Ogene ogene nta
Onye na cho ogene
Ogene ogene nta

When Ify and I are partners, we always seem to bump into the other children, and we make them laugh so much, they fall over like ripe oranges on a stormy day!

HOW TO PLAY

KPU KPUN KPU OGENE

(Oranges and lemons)
For this game, you need 8-14 players, lined up in pairs with their hands joined and raised making a "roof". To win, each pair takes it in turns to try and walk under the roof to the end of the row without touching anyone.

I wonder whether I should choose
Onye ne na anya azu, a chasing game.
But I suppose it's really Amaka's game.
She's another friend of mine. She
moves very fast, and when we sing

> *Onye ne na anya azu*
> *mmonwu anyi na bia na azu*
> *onye ne na anya azu*

anyone who puts the leaves down
behind Amaka had better watch out!
Amaka always catches up with them,
however fast they go. She has eyes at
the back of her head!

What about *Oga,* a copying game?

But every girl I know says it is her favourite game. So I can't choose it, or we'll all end up arguing.

Whenever we play Oga, Papa always knows where we are, because we clap our hands loudly. Then he shouts out, "Hey, children! Can't you think of something a bit quieter to do in this heat?"

HOW TO PLAY

OGA *(A copying game)*

For this game you need 2-10 players standing in a row. To win, a player must copy like a mirror-image whatever the main player does. The main player moves along the row, clapping her hands and kicking out one foot very fast. Each person she faces must copy exactly what she does. If the person she faces does it wrong, she goes on to the next person. But if the person she faces copies her exactly, then she goes out and the new person takes over.

Now I've thought of all the games
I know, and I still can't decide which
is my favourite. What am I going to
tell Ngony?

Mama is worried about me.
She even tries to help by showing me
her favourite game! But I tell her,
"Don't worry, Mama. I'll be all right.
I just need to clear my head. I'll go
to the *ama* and think about it."

Later, while I am sprinkling salt and pepper
on my paper dinner, I have an idea…

Of course I have a favourite game!
I can play it better than all my friends.
It's called *Gathers*.

I run to find a piece of string, tie the ends
together and make the string into a shape called
Aka Odoo (pestle), just like the one Mama
uses in the kitchen for pounding food.

Then I make *Onwa di na atiti uwa*
(the Moon Sitting in the Middle of
the Universe).

Then I make the best shape of all —
I call it Two Pairs of Trousers Worn
by Twins!

Now I'm happy again. I've got
something to show my friends. But
first I'll write to Ngony and tell her
my favourite game!

HOW TO PLAY
GATHERS *(Cat's Cradle)*
*For this game you need 1-4 people. Each person
has a metre of string with the ends knotted to
make a big circle. She loops the string behind
her thumbs and little fingers (see opposite top
photo). Then she starts to gather up the string,
using her fingers and thumbs, to make more
interesting shapes than anyone else.*

THE SONGS IN ENGLISH

RYEMBALAY (Wolof)

If your mother gives you a ....,
If your father gives you a ....,
If your grandmother gives you a ....,
These are the steps that you follow –

This is the place where it's hidden!

(Fill in the gaps with something
you would really like)

OKEREKE OKEREKE (Igbo)

Okereke okereke dun-dun-du-ya-ya,
Okereke okereke dun-dun-du-ya-ya,
Do you want to play this game?
We're going to play the game!

KPU KPUN KPU OGENE (Igbo)

Let's crawl through the passage,
A tiny, tiny passage,
Who is looking for the passage?
A tiny, tiny passage.

ONYE NE NA ANYA AZU (Igbo)

No one must look back!
Our spirits are coming behind us.
No one must look back!

In the Wolof and Igbo songs, you sound out all the vowels.
So ***mmonwu anyi na bia na azu*** is pronounced **mmm-orn-woo an-yee na bee-a na a-zu**,
and ***okereke*** is pronounced **o-ke-re-ke**.

OTHER PICTURE BOOKS IN PAPERBACK FROM FRANCES LINCOLN

A IS FOR AFRICA
Ifeoma Onyefulu

From Beads to Drums to Masquerades, from Grandmother to Yams,
this photographic alphabet captures the rhythms of day-to-day village life in Africa.
Ifeoma Onyefulu's lens reveals not only traditional crafts and customs, but also the African sense
of occasion and fun, in images that will enchant children the world over.
"Delightful and highly original – an enchanting book with a positive and fresh perspective." *Junior Education*

Suitable for National Curriculum Geography, Key Stages 1 and 2; English – Reading, Key Stages 1 and 2
Scottish Guidelines Environmental Studies – Levels B and C; English Language – Reading, Levels B and C
ISBN 0-7112-1029-2 £4.99

EMEKA'S GIFT
Ifeoma Onyefulu

Emeka sets off to visit his grandmother in the next village.
He would like to buy her a special present and on his way he looks at all kinds of things,
from 6 beautiful beaded necklaces to 9 pestles and mortars.
A stunningly photographed counting book, full of information about African life.
"The author is mainly a photographer and a brilliant one too. Out of her love for Nigeria
she has made this outstanding counting book." *Junior Bookshelf*

Suitable for National Curriculum Geography, Key Stages 1 and 2; English – Reading, Key Stages 1 and 2
Scottish Guidelines Environmental Studies, Levels B and C; English Language – Reading, Levels B and C;

Talking and Listening, Level B
ISBN 0-7112-1255-4 £4.99

THE ABOVE TITLES ARE ALSO AVAILABLE IN BIG BOOK FORMAT

Frances Lincoln titles are available from all good bookshops.
Prices are correct at time of publication, but may be subject to change.